BABAR'S
Birthday Surprise

Laurent de Brunhoff

BABAR'S Birthday Surprise

HARRY N. ABRAMS, INC., PUBLISHERS

In the country of the elephants, Podular, the sculptor, was finishing a pretty little statue of his friend King Babar.

But suddenly—*tap! tap! tap!*—someone knocked on the door. Queen Celeste entered with the Old Lady and Cousin Arthur.

When the little statue was finished, Podular went to the door with his visitors. Celeste let Babar walk on ahead with the Old Lady, then turned to speak to the sculptor in a low voice.

"My dear Podular," she said, "I would like to give Babar a surprise for his birthday. Here is my idea. Will you carve a giant

statue of King Babar right in the side of the mountain?"

"Bravo! Bravo!" cried Arthur and Zephir.

Podular was very enthusiastic, too.

"But take care," added Celeste. "Babar must suspect nothing!"

Aided by Zephir, Podular loaded his truck. Without losing a minute, they set off for the mountain.

Finally they found a place where the stone seemed well suited for carving. They cut down some trees and raised scaffolding against the mountain.

Suddenly two marabous perched beside them.

"What are you doing here?" they cried. "We are planning to build our nest on this mountain!"

But when they learned that Podular was going to carve a large statue of Babar in the rock, they clicked their beaks joyously and declared that they were ready to help.

Suddenly, a cry from Zephir interrupted them. "Babar!" he shouted. "Babar is coming this way on his bicycle!"

Podular had forgotten that Babar often took this road to go fishing. Fortunately it led behind the mountain so Babar saw nothing.

But Podular was upset all the same. He called the two marabous.

"Would you be good enough to stand guard?" he asked. "Then I won't have to worry."

Césarine, the giraffe, was very excited by the adventure. She stood watch with the marabous, too.

First Podular carved Babar's crown. Then he began defining one of the eyes with his drill. Suddenly a horn tooted.

"Look out!" cried the giraffe. "It's Babar!"

However, the sculptor did not seem to be worried.

"It's all right, Césarine," he said calmly. "Take a good look."

It was not Babar who was coming at all. Podular and the little monkey had recognized the horn of Arthur's red car. They climbed down to welcome him.

"We are getting along well, aren't we?" Zephir called to him. "You know, Babar just went by."

Arthur couldn't believe his ears. "What? And he saw the statue?"

"Not at all, Arthur," Podular reassured him. "The secret is well kept. Your friend Zephir is nothing but a tease. Now enjoy yourselves, but don't bother me."

The head of the statue was soon finished. Podular began working next on Babar's necktie. "At least the most difficult part is done," he thought.

Suddenly the marabous began to cry out again. "Someone is coming by bicycle!"

Arthur held his breath . . . .

"All is lost," sighed Podular.

But no. Three bicycles—not one—had stopped at the foot of the mountain. Babar's children had come to see the statue.

"Hi, Alexander! Pom! Flora!" Podular called to them. "It is nice of you to come see us."

"Oh! How handsome Papa is as a mountain!" said Alexander.

Finally Podular was nearly finished with his work. He climbed down to carve the feet.

"Time for a picnic!" cried the children.

Back in Celesteville everyone was very busy. Babar's birthday was to be a wonderful celebration. Poutifour, the gardener, watered his flowers.

"I can be proud of my flower beds," he declared.

In the palace kitchens, the Old Lady and Celeste came to see the cooks. No doubt about it, the cakes would be delicious.

Babar and Celeste took a walk together.

Celeste was nervous because Babar was so deep in thought. "Does he suspect something?" she wondered.

But Babar told her that he was upset about losing his pipe the other day when he had gone fishing. Celeste promised herself that she would give him a beautiful new pipe.

Meanwhile, Cornelius rehearsed for the concert to be given on the great day.

On the very top of the mountain, behind the head of the statue, Podular and his friends were enjoying their picnic. They could see the city, the palace, and the river off in the distance. But who was coming up the road by bicycle?

It was Babar! Would the secret be discovered at the last moment?

Flora and Alexander, who were playing below, hid in the underbrush.

"I am looking for my pipe," Babar said to the giraffe. "I wonder if it fell around here? The other day I felt something slip from my pocket, but I didn't pay any attention."

With a flap of their wings, the marabous approached.

"A pipe will be hard to find in such a big place," said one.

"I was just playing with it," said the other. "Now where did I leave it?"

At that very moment, Flora stepped on the pipe.

Hearing the noise, Babar turned around. "What was that?" he asked.

"I am afraid I just stepped on your pipe," one of the marabous answered quickly.

Immediately, the two birds brought Babar the pieces of his pipe, while Flora and Alexander tried to make themselves small behind the bushes.

"Ah, thank you, gentlemen," exclaimed Babar. "I really love this pipe. I will glue it together again."

“Saved! Babar did not see the statue!” cried the children. In their joy, they jumped wildly about on the scaffolding.

“Stop that, you little mischiefs!” scolded Podular. Too late—one board slid, and then the whole scaffold collapsed!

What a fall! They were all a little stunned.

"Arthur has hurt his trunk," said the sculptor. "We must go fetch Doctor Capoulosse."

Zephir jumped into the red car and drove off. In no time at all, he returned with the doctor.

Capoulosse examined Arthur. "It is not serious," he said. He cleaned the wound and then he gently rolled a long bandage around the trunk.

"I think it would be a good idea to take him back to Celesteville for a little rest," he added.

"Oh! Doctor, you won't say anything to Babar, will you?" asked Arthur nervously.

"No, no, little one, don't worry. I will not say a word."

Left alone with Zephir, Podular tidied up all his tools and his ladders. Then he called the marabous.

"Dear friends," he said. "Tomorrow is Babar's birthday. Will you ask the birds to hide the statue until the signal is given? Cornelius will lead a joyous fanfare."

The following day a crowd of elephants headed toward the mountain. Babar was very happy.

"How nice of you, Celeste, to organize this celebration! I love to lunch on the grass."

Celeste smiled. She was thinking that soon Babar would be even happier.

As they drew near, Babar saw millions of birds covering the mountainside. The view was very beautiful. Astonished, he asked, "Are they part of the festival, too?"

"Of course," Celeste answered. "They came just for your birthday. Everybody wanted to come. For, as you will see, there is a surprise. . . ."

"Oh, yes, a surprise," repeated Cornelius as he trotted away.

Cornelius assembled the musicians of the Royal Guard. One! Two! Three! The trumpets sounded the fanfare. At this signal, all the birds covering the mountain flew up at the same time. The air was filled with the loud fluttering of wings.

Babar was stupefied. “Why, it’s me! Extraordinary!” he said, hugging Celeste. “What a splendid statue. Podular, my friend, I congratulate you. Dear Celeste, I am very moved. What an enormous surprise!”

After lunch, the cooks from the palace brought out an enormous cake.

"Happy birthday!" the children shouted.

Then Cornelius said, "Babar, it is up to you to cut the cake."

"Oh, yes, quickly," added Arthur, sounding funny because of the bandage on his trunk.

Everyone cried, "Happy birthday! Happy birthday!"

Except for the weary Podular, who was fast asleep.

DESIGNER, ABRAMS EDITION: BECKY TERHUNE

The artwork for each picture is prepared using watercolor on paper.
This text is set in 16-point Comic Sans.

Library of Congress Cataloging-in-Publication Data

Brunhoff, Laurent de.
[Anniversaire de Babar. English]
Babar's birthday surprise / by Laurent de Brunhoff.
p. cm.
Summary: Queen Celeste decides to surprise King Babar with a statue of himself for his birthday but has a difficult time keeping it a secret.
ISBN 0-8109-5713-2
[1. Elephants--Fiction.]
I. Title.
PZ7.B82843 Babiu 2002
[E]--dc21

2001003741

First published in 1970. Published in 2002 by Harry N. Abrams, Incorporated, New York

PRINTED AND BOUND IN BELGIUM

10 9 8 7 6 5 4 3 2 1

Harry N. Abrams, Inc.
100 Fifth Avenue
New York, N.Y. 10011
www.abramsbooks.com

Abrams is a subsidiary of